A POMSKY PUBLISHING PRODUCTION

This Book Belongs To

_____

_____

Color Test Page

A BIG THANK YOU!

SCAN ME⬚

If you enjoyed this book could you kindly leave us a review?

A BIG
THANK YOU!

SCAN ME

If you enjoyed this book could you kindly leave us a review?

Made in the USA
Monee, IL
27 August 2024

64512523R00063